INSTRUMENTAL PLAY-ALONG

Trumpet

CHRISTMAS FAVOURITES

Contents

HOW TO USE THE CD ACCOMPANIMENT:
A melody cue appears on the right channel only. If your CD player has a balance   you can adjust the volume
of the melody by turning down the right channel.

This publication is not authorised for sale in the United States of America and/or Canada

Exclusive Distributors:
Music Sales Limited
14-15 Berners Street, London W1T 3LJ, UK.

Order No. HLE90003267
ISBN: 978-1-84772-317-8
This book © Copyright 2007 Hal Leonard Europe

Printed in the USA

Your Guarantee of Quality
As publishers, we strive to produce every book to the highest commercial standards. The book has been carefully designed to minimise awkward page turns and to make playing from it a real pleasure. Throughout, the printing and binding have been planned to ensure a sturdy, attractive publication which should give years of enjoyment. If your copy fails to meet our high standards, please inform us and we will gladly replace it.

www.musicsales.com

HAL LEONARD EUROPE
DISTRIBUTED BY MUSIC SALES

◆ BLUE CHRISTMAS

TRUMPET

Words and Music by BILLY HAYES
and JAY JOHNSON

❷ CAROLING, CAROLING

TRUMPET

Words by WIHLA HUTSON
Music by ALFRED BURT

❸ FELIZ NAVIDAD

TRUMPET

Music and Lyrics by
JOSÉ FELICIANO

◆ FROSTY THE SNOWMAN

Words and Music by
STEVE NELSON and JACK ROLLINS

TRUMPET

◆5 HAPPY XMAS
(War Is Over)

TRUMPET

Words and Music by JOHN LENNON
and YOKO ONO

◆ 6 HERE COMES SANTA CLAUS
(Right Down Santa Claus Lane)

TRUMPET

Words and Music by GENE AUTRY
and OAKLEY HALDEMAN

(There's No Place Like)
❼ HOME FOR THE HOLIDAYS

TRUMPET

Words by AL STILLMAN
Music by ROBERT ALLEN

❽ IT'S BEGINNING TO LOOK LIKE CHRISTMAS

TRUMPET

By MEREDITH WILLSON

JINGLE BELL ROCK

Words and Music by
JOE BEAL and JIM BOOTHE

TRUMPET

50's Rock & Roll

LET IT SNOW! LET IT SNOW! LET IT SNOW!

Words by SAMMY CAHN
Music by JULE STYNE

TRUMPET

⑪ LITTLE SAINT NICK

TRUMPET

Words and Music by BRIAN WILSON
and MIKE LOVE

⬥12 MERRY CHRISTMAS, DARLING

TRUMPET

Words and Music by RICHARD CARPENTER
and FRANK POOLER

◆13 MY FAVOURITE THINGS

From THE SOUND OF MUSIC

Lyrics by OSCAR HAMMERSTEIN II
Music by RICHARD RODGERS

TRUMPET

SANTA BABY

TRUMPET

By JOAN JAVITS,
PHIL SPRINGER and TONY SPRINGER

◆ SILVER BELLS

From the Paramount Motion Picture THE LEMON DROP KID

Words and Music by
JAY LIVINGSTON and RAY EVANS

TRUMPET